AMAZON ORIGINAL

Tumble Leaf

The Bumpy, Thumpy Bedtime

Adapted by Lara Bergen

Text based on the episode "Things That Go Gourd In The Night" written by Karl Geurs.

© 2017 Amazon Content Services LLC.
Tumble Leaf © 2013–2017 Amazon Content Services LLC.

Published by Two Lions, New York

www.apub.com

Amazon, the Amazon logo, and Two Lions are trademarks of Amazon.com, Inc., or its affiliates.

ISBN-13: 9781503946675 (paperback)
ISBN-10: 1503946673 (paperback)

Book design by Tanya Ross-Hughes

Printed in China

two lions

Late one night in Tumble Leaf, Fig and his best friend, Stick, were fast asleep. At least they *were* until the *jingle-jangle* of the chimes outside Fig's window woke them.

"Brrrrlllll!" said Stick. He and Fig both
knew what that sound meant.

"Something new is in the Finding Place!" said Fig.
"But at *this* time of night?"

They hurried to it. "I wonder what we'll find tonight?" Fig asked.

Inside the Finding Place was
a notebook—and a pencil, too!
"This'll be great for drawing
stuff," Fig said.

"*Brrrrlllll!*" Stick agreed.

Fig rubbed his eyes and yawned a sleepy yawn. "Not now, though. In the morning. Let's go back to sleep."

But just as they were leaving . . . **Bump.**

Thump!

They stopped and looked up.
"Brrlllllll!" exclaimed Stick.

"*Whoaaaaa!*" gasped Fig.

"I wonder what's making that sound?"

Fig and Stick turned the corner and backed right into . . .

. . . their friends Zucchini and Rutabaga and their chicks, Butternut and Squash. The chickens had heard the sound, too.

Bump-Thump!
Thump-Bump-Thump!

There it was again!
What was making that noise?

"*Brrll*," said Stick.

"What's that, Stick?" asked Fig. "You think you know what the sound is?"

"*Brrrrrllllllll!*" said Stick, waving his arms.

Fig opened the notebook. "Okay! You say what you hear, Stick, and I'll draw it . . . ," he declared.

"*Brrrll, brrrrlllllll, brrrll,*" Stick told Fig.
"You think it's the dreaded pirate Captain Centipede?!" Fig exclaimed.
He started to draw faster as Stick went on.
"*Brrrrllll, brrrlllll, brrllll, brrrrllllllll!*" said Stick.

Bump-Thump-Thump!

rumbled down from above.

"And that *thumpety-bumpety* sound we hear
is Captain Centipede banging into things with all
his wooden legs because he has two eye patches
and can't see?" Fig turned to the others.
"C'mon! Let's see if Stick is right!"
Fig led his friends up onto the deck.

"Oh, Mr. Piiiraaate . . . ," he called,
glancing around.

Thump-Thump!

"*Whoa!*" The next thing Fig knew he had stepped into a couple of buckets.

*"Thump and shout,
I figured it out!"*

"There's no Captain Centipede bumping into things. . . . It was just these buckets!" Fig said. "The wind must have knocked them over. Now that we know what the sound was we can all go back to sleep." Fig yawned, while Stick *brrrlled* sleepily.

Just then— **Baroomp! Ribbit.**

The chickens' eyes grew wide. So did Fig's and Stick's.
"Wait! Did you hear *that*? I think it's coming from *that* way," said Fig,
pointing toward the woods.

Baroomp! Ribbit. They heard it again.

"We're not gonna get any sleep," said Fig, "till we figure out what it is."

And so they jumped into Zucchini's cart and rolled toward
the woods. The friends stopped in Froggy Bog at the rocky wall.
Fig's friend Maple was already there in her pajamas—
she couldn't sleep either because of all the noise.

Baroomp!

"Creepy critters!" said Fig.
"What do you think it could be?"

Ribbit.

"Wait a minute!" Maple said.
"I know what it is!"

Fig quickly got out his notebook. "*Rumble Leaf, Tumble Leaf!*
Maple, you say what you hear and I'll draw it!"
"It's the Star-Hopping Frog Bug!" said Maple.

"She *boomity-hops* all night—higher than the moon!—making sounds like . . ."

Baroomp! Ribbit.

". . . like *that!*" Maple declared.

"You think that Star-Hopping Frog Bug made that *baroomp* sound?" said Fig.

"Um . . . I think so . . . ," said Maple.

"Only one way to know for sure," Fig said as he finished his sketch.

"C'mon! Let's follow the sound!"

"*Ribbit,*" croaked a frog when the cart pulled up.
"Oh, Maple! You have a really big *baroomping*
imagination. It must have been this frog making
the sound we heard," Fig laughed.
"I've always had a great imagination!" Maple laughed, too.

Arooo! Arooo!

Fig and his friends all spun around.
"What was *that* sound?" Maple asked.

Hmm . . . , Fig thought. It sounded like something he'd heard before. . . .
The friends rolled on to Beetle Hollow, trying to follow the sound.
But Beetle Hollow was empty.

"Whatever or whoever made that sound, it's not here." Maple sighed.
"But it looks like it *was*!" Fig said, pointing to a pod with a big dent.

"Who do we know," said Fig, "who's big enough to make a dent like that *and* likes to go '*Arooooo*!'?"

He drew a quick sketch
and showed his friends.

*"Turtle trout,
I figured it out!"*

"Get the picture?
It's *Gourd*!" he said.

The friends hurried toward the noise, and found Gourd dancing
and *Arooo-hoo-hooing* in his sleep.
"Gourd . . . wake up . . . ," Fig said gently.

Gourd stopped thumping and bouncing
and *Aroooing.* "Oh, hello, Fig," he said.
"What am I doing out of bed?"

Fig couldn't help but chuckle.
"*Brrrllll, brrlll, brrrllllll!*" Stick giggled, too.
They realized it had been *Gourd*
who had sleepwalked into the buckets
and sleep-*thumped* all over the deck.

And it had been *Gourd* who
had sleep-danced to Froggy Bog

and *baroomped*
and bounced from log to log!

Everyone was happy to have solved the **bumpy-thumpy** mystery.

"I figured out something else, too," Fig said. "Our *imaginations*
were even *bigger* than the sounds we heard!"
"Good figurin', Fig!" cheered Maple.

At last! Everyone could go back to sleep . . . and that's just what they did.